SANDY, TOSH AND THE MOO COW

BY PAULA-ANNE PORTER JONES

Blue Banyan Books

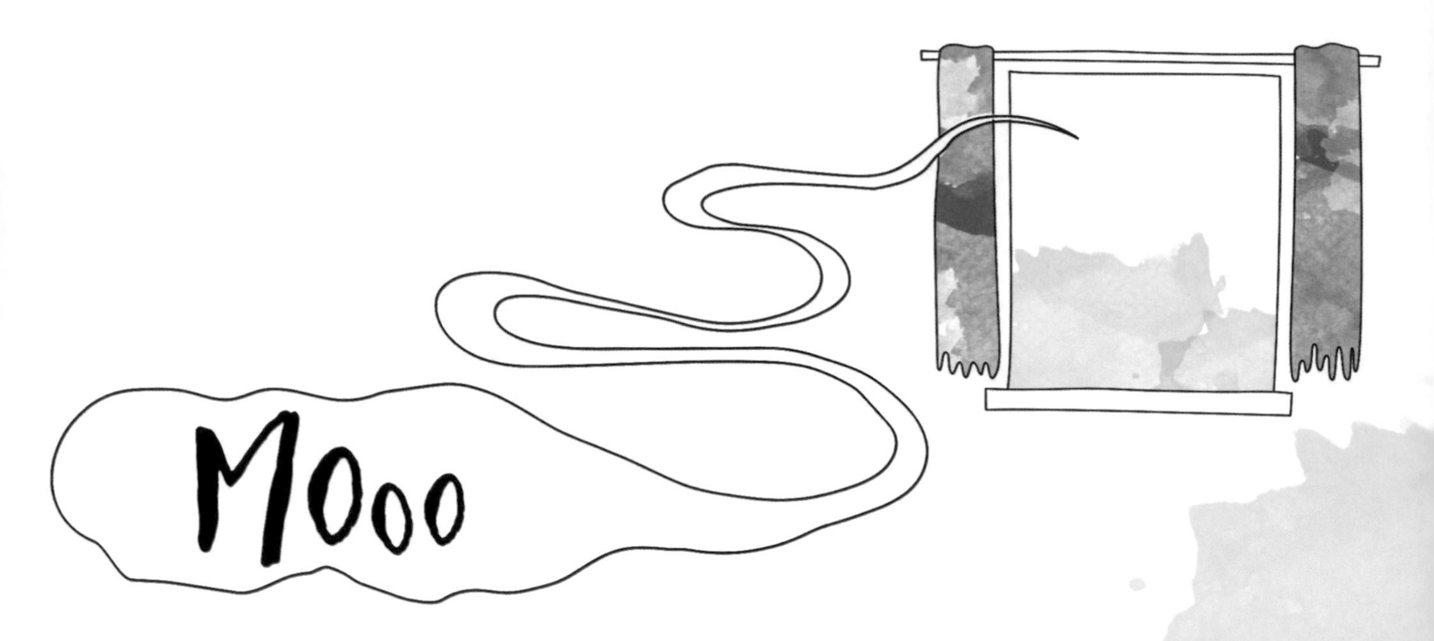

One morning Tosh awoke to loud moos outside.

He jumped out of bed
and called for his big sister.

Sandy and Tosh ran to the window and peered out just in time to see

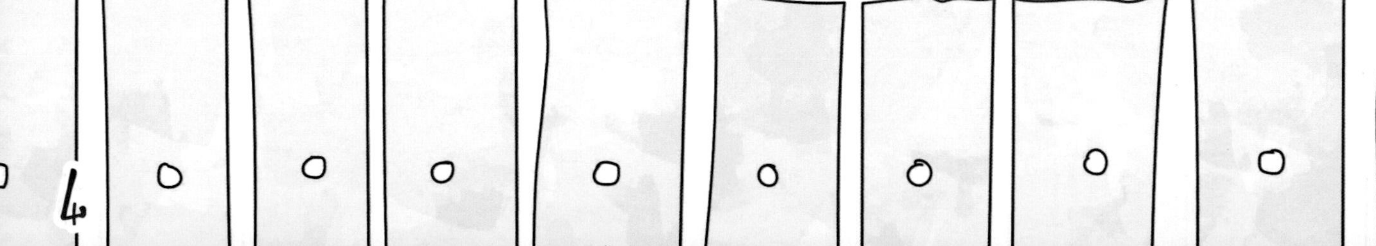

the swish of a brown tail
disappearing down the street.

Tosh wanted to see more.
"Sandy, Sandy, Moo cow!" Tosh said jumping up and down.

"Hmmm. Ok. Let's go on an early morning adventure," said Sandy.

"Just be careful
and don't get
too close,"
Mommy said.

Sandy and Tosh
headed up the road.
They saw

four lizards, three cats,
two chickens, and
lots of grasshoppers -
but no cows.

So, they turned around
and headed down the road.

They saw yellow birds,
pink flowers, grey rats,
lots of green grass
and -

"Moo cows!"

Tosh was very, very happy.

He saw the
big brown eyes.

He saw the
long
swishy
tail.

He saw the
pointy ears.

He saw the big, sharp teeth...

Wait a minute!

cows don't have
big, sharp teeth.

Oh No!

It was a huge, scary dog and he was about to chase one of the cows.

And that cow
was about to run
toward Tosh and Sandy

who very smartly decided
to run home.

They got there
just in time
to close the gate,

and lock out the lizards, cats,
grasshoppers, rats, chickens,
birds, big, scary dog,

and brown Moo cows.

THE END

Published by Blue Banyan Books Ltd.

Art and Book Design by Ion Communications Ltd.

PO Box 5464, Liguanea PO
Kingston 6, Jamaica, WI

www.bluebanyanbooks.com

ISBN 978-976-8267-14-6